This book belongs to

....

....

GW Publishing

www.gwpublishing.com

This is Hamish the haggis
of the McHaggis clan,
rarely seen by
the eyes of man.

Hamish

Rupert Harold the Third
is an English gent,
travelling far from
his home in Kent.

Rupert

Our Jeannie's an osprey with wide sweeping wings,
who is easily distracted by all sorts of things.

Jeannie

Angus

Young Angus is cheeky and likes playing the fool,
whatever he's doing he's got to look cool.

For Carlo
with love. L.S.

For Sarah
with love. S.J.C.

Text and Illustrations copyright © Linda Strachan and Sally J. Collins

www.hamishmchaggis.co.uk
www.lindastrachan.com

First published in paperback in Great Britain 2006
Reprinted 2007, 2011 and 2015

The rights of Linda Strachan and Sally J. Collins to be identified
as the author and illustrator of this work have been asserted by them
in accordance with the Copyright, Designs and Patents Act 1988

Design - Veneta Hooper

Reprographics - GWP Graphics

Printed in China

Published by

GW Publishing
PO Box 6091
Thatcham
Berks
RG19 8XZ

Tel +44 (0) 1635 268080
www.gwpublishing.com

ISBN 09551564-0-8
978-09551564-0-3

Hamish McHaggis

and
The Wonderful Water Wheel

By Linda Strachan

Illustrated by Sally J. Collins

"Where's Angus?" asked Hamish. "It's lunch time and I've not seen him all morning. Is he still away doon the burn?"

"Doon the burn?" Rupert looked concerned.

Jeannie looked up from her maps and gave a little laugh.

"C'mon, Rupert, I'll show you."

"Don't be long," said Hamish. "Lunch is almost ready."

"We won't," grinned Rupert. "It's my favourite, Apple Crunchie, and it looks particularly good today!"

Rupert followed Jeannie behind the McHaggis Hoggle
and down the hill towards a small stream.
"See," she said, pointing with her wing. "That's the
burn. It's a stream."

"What's wrong, Angus? I thought you'd be having fun."
Jeannie turned to Rupert. "Doesn't he look miserable?"
"I can't sail my boats down safely to this bit of the burn,"
Angus moaned.
"What about a canal?" Rupert asked Angus. "That could be
a way to get your boats down to the other part of the . . .
the burn!"
"What's a canal?" asked Angus.
"Well, a canal is..."

Jeannie saw Hamish waving at
them from the top of the hill.
"We'd better get back to the Hoggle for lunch,
Rupert. You can explain it to him there."
So Angus picked his boats out of the burn and followed
Rupert and Jeannie back up the hill.

After lunch Rupert started to explain what a canal was. "A canal has locks and gates," he told Angus.

Angus giggled. "I can't see how a gate will help in a river, the water would run right through it, and I don't think a lock would help one wee bit."

"I have an idea," said Hamish. "Have you heard of the Falkirk Wheel?"

"No," Angus shook his head. "What does it do?"

"It takes boats up in the air so that they can reach another canal higher up the hill." Hamish showed them a picture. "Why don't we take a ride on a canal boat and we can go up on the Falkirk Wheel, too."

"It looks a bit scary," Angus said, wide-eyed.

"Not at all," grinned Hamish. "It will be great fun."

"I'll take my captain's hat and my whistle and I'd better take my boat."

"I think I'll take my new telescope and I'll pack a picnic too. We may get a wee bit hungry."

They set off happily, singing and playing Spot the Highland Cow, but very soon they came to a crossroads. Hamish stopped the Whirry Bang and climbed out.

"We're lost!" he said.

"I'm sure it's that way, Hamish." Jeannie pointed with her wing, back the way they had come.

Rupert shook his head. "No, Jeannie, it's this way."

Angus swung out of the Whirry Bang. "Look! A tattie bogle! He's pointing that way!"

"What?" Rupert spun around expecting to see some strange beast. Hamish burst out laughing. He climbed up onto the Whirry Bang. "Look! I think I can see the Falkirk Wheel. Rupert, you were right, that is the way."

"Harrumph!" said Rupert, trying to hide his smile.

Bang!
Whirr!

When they arrived at the canal the boat was waiting.
"All aboard!" the Captain shouted.
They all pushed and heaved until the Whirry Bang was
safely on board.
"Let's go, Captain!" Angus called out.
With a

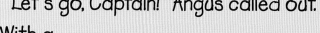

chug and a
rumble

the engines started and the canal boat moved
forward past the huge lock gates until they
were in the lock.

Chug!
Chug!

Slowly the gates closed behind them.
"This is exciting!" gasped Angus. "Look
how tall the lock gates are."

Very gently the water level rose, lifting the boat
higher and higher inside the lock until they could just
see over the top of the lock gates.

The captain leapt off the boat, turned the wheel and
then he pulled hard on the lever to open the gates in
front of them. He jumped back onto the boat

and they sailed on down the canal.

The huge silvery metal wheel shone in the sunshine. It was moving slowly round, carrying boats up in an enormous cradle full of water.. "Jings!" said Angus, as he leapt off the boat. "Is that the Falkirk Wheel? It's **enormous**."
Hamish grinned as he helped himself to a sweet, crunchy apple.

"Look!" said Jeannie. "There's a tunnel up at the top."

   "We'll soon be going up on the wheel and through that tunnel, Jeannie," said Rupert, peering at a leaflet. "According to this we will sail into a long bucket full of water and we'll be lifted to the top. Fascinating!"

The canal boat sailed
into the pond at the foot of
the wheel and once the cradle gate
was closed behind them the wheel started
turning, taking them up higher and higher until
they were at the top. They sailed along through the
tunnel and then their boat stopped to turn around.

"It wasn't scary at all," grinned Angus. He blew his whistle as the boat sailed back through the tunnel. "Do we go down on the wheel again?"

Hamish took out his telescope. "Yes, Angus, it takes us back again."

Rupert looked down at the countryside below them. "We can see for miles and miles from up here."

"Mmmh," muttered Jeannie, peering into the water looking for fish.

The next day Hamish was looking at Rupert's photographs of their trip. "That's a braw picture!"

"Yes," agreed Rupert. "And isn't that a good one of Jeannie on the boat? What do you think, Jeannie?"

But Jeannie was so busy looking at her maps that she didn't even hear him.

There was a hammering noise coming from the back room. "Angus is fair working up a lather in there. He'll be puggled!" Hamish declared.

"He'll be what?" asked Rupert.

"Puggled! He'll be tired out," Hamish translated. "I wonder what he's making?"

Bang! Bang!

Bang! Bang!

That afternoon Angus asked everyone to come down to the burn.
"What is it?" Jeannie asked, staring at the contraption Angus
had built.

   "It's my Wonderful Water Wheel! My own version of the
Falkirk Wheel," Angus announced proudly. "It will move my boats
safely from up there to down here."

Rupert took a photograph of Angus and his invention. "Well done, Angus. It's grand!"

"What's the matter?" Hamish asked Jeannie later that day. "You keep staring at your maps. I didn't think you would need maps. You fly all the way from here to Africa and back again every year and you never seem to get lost."

Jeannie frowned. "When I fly I can see where I am, so I don't get lost. But how can you tell where you are on a map? It's so flat."

Hamish showed Jeannie how to read the map. "These wee blue lines are rivers," he explained. "And the red and yellow ones are roads. There's also a key. That's what you call the bit that tells you what all the different symbols and colours mean. Here's the key at the side."

Jeannie fluttered her wings. "How clever. But I still can't find Coorie Doon. All the other places have their names on the map."

Hamish laughed. "You'll not find Coorie Doon on the map, Jeannie. Otherwise it wouldn't be a **secret** glen, would it?"

DID YOU KNOW?

Coorie Doon means to nestle or cosy down comfortably.

A burn is a small stream.

A tattie bogle is a scarecrow.

Working up a lather means working hard at something.

To be puggled means to be exhausted.

Braw means good.

Jings! is an exclamation of surprise.

It is commonly thought that a **Haggis** has three legs, two long and one short. Hamish gets a fit of the giggles when he hears this.

Angus is a Pine Marten.

Pine Martens have hairy soles on their feet which stop them slipping when it is icy.

Hedgehogs can roll into a ball to protect themselves from harm.

Osprey eggs are white, pink or cream coloured, with brown splotches.

The **Falkirk Wheel** is the world's only rotating boatlift. It connects the Forth & Clyde and Union canals in central Scotland.

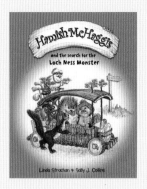

**Hamish McHaggis
and The Search for The
Loch Ness Monster**

978-0-9546701-5-3

**Hamish McHaggis
and The Edinburgh Adventure**

978-0-9546701-7-7

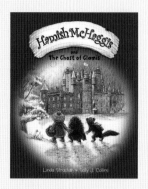

**Hamish McHaggis
and The Ghost of Glamis**

978-0-9546701-9-1

**Hamish McHaggis
and The Skye Surprise**

978-0-9546701-8-4

**Hamish McHaggis
and The Skirmish at Stirling**

978-0-9551564-1-0

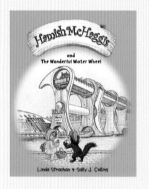

**Hamish McHaggis
and The Wonderful Water Wheel**

978-0-9551564-0-3

**Hamish McHaggis
and The Wonderful Water Wheel**

978-0-9554145-5-8

**Hamish McHaggis
and The Clan Gathering**

978-0-9561211-2-7

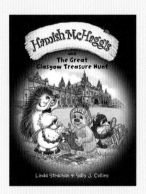

**Hamish McHaggis
and The Great
Glasgow Treasure Hunt**

978-0-9570844-0-7

**Hamish McHaggis
Activity and Story Book**

978-0-9554145-1-0

Also by the
same author
and illustrator

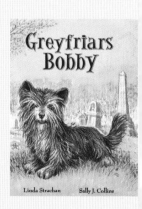

Greyfriars Bobby

978-0-9551564-2-7